MW01244782

HIDDEN DESIRES

Shalya's Story

C. A. LUV

Hard Drive Publishing

St. Louis Missouri

1

H.D. Campbell Productions

St. Louis Missouri

First Printing

ISBN: 9798543197066

PUBLISHED BY HARD DRIVE BOOK PUBLISHERS

www.harddrivepublishing.com

COVER BY DELON ANOSHI HAGOOD

www.queenanosi.com

Printed in the United States of America

dication

First, I would like to give God thanks for giving me the wisdom knowledge and ability to ite my first book. I have been told for years that there was a book in me that needed to come rth and here is the first of many. Thank you to my husband and best friend Derrick for giving e the space to sit still and write, for encouraging me to keep it going. Thank you to my six ildren, my FWO (for women only) group, my church family Truth Foundation Outreach nistry, and the inspiration that I got from my past. I am truly encouraged…. Special thanks to cousin Delon Anoshi she inspires me more then she would ever know!! I love everyone and I ay this book speaks to you the way it did to me! ENJOY!

The phone rings...

Shalay: Hello.

Chelle: You busy?

Shalay: No, I am just relaxing.

Chelle: Meet me.

Shalay: Are you crazy? My husband is here.

Chelle: I need to see you so bad.

Shalay: (Inhales deeply.) Where?

Chelle: Our usual spot.

Shalay: Ok, but briefly...

Later that evening at the usual spot, the sound of lovemaking filled the air.

"Oh God Chelle, you make me feel so good," moaned Shalay

"Don't be so loud," Chelle replied quietly. "Someone is going to hear us."

"Shalay spread that booty for me," Chelle commanded. "YES! Just like that...aww that pussy is beautiful, it's making my mouth drool."

Chelle then whispered commands.

"Chelle sit on my face. That's my favorite position! Those tits are so perky and voluptuous."

"So are yours Sha..."

"Aww gosh! I'm going to cum!" Chelle interrupted in pure passion. "Let's do it togeth sha..."

Wait...I guess you are wondering what is going on here. Well let's start from the beginning, shall we?

Spending the night out with friends was the norm in our neighborhood. Being able to ve company over or be someone's company was the most exciting time we would have in the mmer. One particular night, Liz and Ann came over. We talked for hours until there was a ock on the door.   It was our new neighbors who moved in about two months ago. Liz met r already so she introduced her to everyone else.

"Michelle this is Ann and this is Shalay."

My eyes were gazed like I was in a trance. She was beautiful and had a nice body with obs to die for, I was staring so hard, I didn't even realize she was talking to me.

"Hi Shalay it's nice to meet you," said Michelle. "Is everything okay?"

"Uhhh umm yes, I am sorry my mind wandered off a bit. Nice to meet you, have a seat. e you going to be staying over with us this weekend?"

I hoped she would say yes.

"Yes Shalay, if it is okay with everyone."

Everyone agreed and said yes.

We all sat up until 11p.m. and eventually everyone started to fall asleep except for chelle and I. We continued our conversation until midnight. As soon as she started to doze f, I watched her drift until she fell completely asleep. I undressed her with my eyes and mind.

Wait a minute...this isn't right. We are only 16 years old and should only be thinking out guys NOT girls. Is there something mentally wrong with me? Should I be having these ds of thoughts? Of course not.

Why can't I just fall asleep? My mind continuously raced.

"Oh lord Shalay...snap out of it!" I whispered to myself, as I watch her turn over.

"Hey Shalay, why are you still up?" Michelle asked. "It's late."

Michelle continued, "Why don't you get some rest? We are heading over to the mall morrow."

"Okay Michelle, I am going to lay down now."

"Well lay down next to me Sha."

My heart is now pounding with my mind spinning.

"Sure Michelle, I can do that."

I laid in complete silence as Michelle turned and faced me in her sleep. **WOW**! This wa going to be a long night. Then, it happened. She put her arms around me and without hesitation. My arms went across her waist. She pulled me closer and my arms began to rub he shoulders and then her back. Michelle moaned and then opened her eyes and smiled. Immediately I saw her lips coming towards mine. We both closed our eyes and began to kiss one another. Her lips were so soft, the kiss was gentle and felt amazing. My eyes went down t those beautiful breasts that were so erect and ready. Michelle removed her shirt and pulled m hands to her round firm breasts. I began to caress them then I rubbed her nipples in a circular motion. I then began to lick and suck those beautiful melons until Michelle moaned louder.

I signaled for her to quiet down so we won't wake the others. Her hands slipped under my nightgown just to find out I wasn't wearing any panties. She began to rub and make my pussy wetter than it already was. Then before I knew it Michelle stuck her finger in my hole. I whimpered with pleasure as she began to move in and out of me faster and faster. So, I happi returned the favor to her. We kissed and fingered each other until we got to that moment of climaxing! We fell asleep wrapped in each other's arms and juices...

"Good morning Liz," Ann welcomed as Liz walked into the kitchen.

When Liz came down, Ann and Sha were already talking.

"Hey Ann, how did you guys sleep?"

"It was so peaceful in our guest room Sha. I could just live here forever."

Yes, it was awesome," said Liz.

Ann apologized, "We didn't mean to leave you alone with the new girl. Hope it was ok."

Sha smiled, "Oh it was just fine."

 "We were just too tired to stay awake with you guys. By the way, where is Michelle, a?"

Sha replied, "I think she was in the shower when I left the room because I heard the ater running."

Michelle entered the room upon hearing her name.

Everyone smiled and said good morning to Chelle!

"Well good morning ladies, that is such a great morning welcome!"

I had my back turned making my breakfast so Michelle gave me a separate hello.

"Good morning Sha, how was your rest?"

"Ohh it was amazing! I am so glad you girls could come over for the weekend!"

My eyes went straight to Chelle as I asked if she wanted anything for breakfast.

With a big grin on her face Chelle replied, "Of course."

Chelle paused and then said, "Oh I will just have eggs and toast, thank you."

Chapter 2

Everyone had just walked in the door after a long Saturday of shopping at the mall.

Sha asked, "Hey Liz, how do you like this new outfit I picked up at the mall?"

"It's too cute Sha! What shoes are you going to wear with it?"

"Well, I have my all-white shell toe adidas."

"Yesss that will be fresh Sha."

"So, what did you get, Liz?"

"I got this blue jean jumper with my sneakers."

"Okay girl," says Sha

"That is all THAT girl!" Liz complimented before addressing Ann, "So, Ann did you find the shoes you were looking for?"

"Yes," Ann said as she pulled her shoes out of the box. "So, what y'all think?"

Everyone spoke out in favor of the shoes.

Ann then personally addressed, "So, Sha what do you think?"

"I really like those, boo!" says Sha. "Hey excuse me girls, I am going to take a shower first. You all take too long for me to get dressed."

I raced to the shower. When I turned the water on and could hear the girls laughing wi **Soul Train** playing on the TV. The shower door opened and there stood Chelle, naked and perky.

My face automatically smiled, but my mouth said, "What are you doing? Liz and Ann a right next door."

"It's okay Sha, they're practicing their dance moves for later."

"Chelle, I don't think this is safe. We could get caught."

"Well Sha if you are not loud, they won't know a damn thing."

So Chelle climbed in and we began to kiss and rub one another! Chelle's hands felt so good against my girly parts, and I immediately opened my legs.

"Sha, can I try something new?"

8

"Well, Chelle we're already this far, I'm sure it won't hurt."

Then it happened! Slowly opening my eyes, I watched as Chelle got on her knees and gan to spread my legs apart. She inserted one finger and then two. I could feel her fingers so ep in my pussy that I began to shed a tear of passion.

She then looked up at me with a smile and then began licking and sucking till my knees re weak. I couldn't stand anymore holding it in and I moaned and groaned and didn't even nk about Liz and Ann hearing me.

It was fantastic! I had someone in my life that made me feel so good and no one knew out our secret. We planned to take this to the grave or at least try to.

Chapter 3

1991

It was a few months before our senior graduation. Liz, Ann, Chelle and Sha were still as close as ever! Liz and Ann had no idea what had taken place between Sha and Chelle every weekend, and they kept it that way.

Liz announced, "Well ladies, it's official we have completed high school!"

"Yaaay," screamed all the girls.

Liz continued, "Our next journey is right ahead of us. Let's go out and PARTY tonight!! We can meet up at the club around 10pm."

Sure thing," said Ann,

"See you there," said Sha.

Our last night together was so awesome. We partied and danced all night long. It was bittersweet because we knew at some point, we were all going our separate ways.

"Hey Chelle can I talk to you?

"Sure," said Sha, "What's up?"

"I just wanted to let you know that I really enjoyed our time together. You have a spac in my heart that I will never replace. I will miss you most of all. I want you to keep in touch wit me no matter what."

Chelle replied, "Absolutely Sha, we can call each other monthly to stay up to date with our lives. I have deep feelings for you so bad I have to suppress them."

"It's ok Chelle, I feel the same way. See you soon."

They both hugged and kissed each other goodbye.

This has been some great college years. I met the guy of dreams. We started dating phomore year and have been together since. We have plans to get married in three months. I n so excited about our wedding day and I just can't wait!

Phill is an engineer and has already bought us a house out in **Manor Hill**. It sits on 5.5 res, with a great view of the ocean. It has fruit trees on both sides he planted himself last ar knowing how much I love fresh fruits. Five bedrooms four and a half bathrooms, a chef's eam kitchen, pool, spa room which includes a sauna, and a three-car garage! Everything I uld dream of or even ask for...or is it?

WEDDING DAY

"Sha, are you ready?" my mom asked.

"Ready as I ever will be, this should be the best day of my life!"

Ann and Liz were able to make it and both be my maid of honor. The cake was gorgeous, my dress fit perfectly, but seeing the girls only made me think about Chelle, my **hidden desire**. Oh, how I missed her and what we shared.

Oh wow, I have to shake myself. I am getting married to a wonderful man in less than two hours,

"Get yourself together Sha," I said to myself.

The wedding was exquisite, we danced our first dance to *Here and Now* by Luther Vandross. We received wonderful gifts and Phill even had a horse and carriage waiting outside to take us to the airport. We were leaving for Hawaii on a late flight, so we went straight to the airport after the reception. Our honeymoon was great, I couldn't ask for it to be any better than it was. Phill and I discussed way before getting married that we would wait at least three years before having children.

He and I both wanted to enjoy one another, the freedom of walking around naked at home, and the sporadic trips we would take! It was fine with me, seeing as I work out every day to keep this coke bottle shape in place!

"Hey Shalay!"

I secretly love when he calls my whole name.

"Yes, my love?"

"I have to take a business trip for about a month. Do you think you will be fine home alone while I am away?"

"Yes, honey I will be fine."

Since I worked from home it was fine. Phill had me an office built right next to the house. All you had to do was walk across a small bridge that was connected to our house, and there you were, right in my office space. I loved not having to drive in the hectic traffic.

My loves Ann and Liz are coming to town soon. Maybe I will ask them to switch some days around and come and stay over like old times.

"That's why I love you Shalay, you make life easy for us."

"I love you too Phill, you created that easy life, so I appreciate *you*. When are you leaving?"

"In two days," Phill said.

"Wow so soon, I asked.

"Yes, my love, it was definitely last minute."

Well, Phill, guess we better go upstairs and do what we do!"

We raced up the stairs and I headed straight for the shower. I could see Phill undressing rough the glass shower walls. He's 6'3 medium built, muscles everywhere and clean shaved th a sexy goatee. I just love the way that goatee feels during oral sex, those hairs would tickle y girly parts and that alone would make me cum. He got into the shower grabbed the loofah d began to wash my back, then he slowly turned me to face him and he began to wash my ontal area, paying close attention to my size 40 Double D's he just loved the way they stood even without a bra on.

After washing my body, he grabbed the shower head to rinse the soap off of me. He atched as the suds washed away and when it was all clear, he kissed me with such passion at it nearly took my breath away. His tongue moved up and down my neck and eased to my s, where he grabbed and sucked them real hard, just the way I liked it. I could feel myself tting wetter and wetter by the minute.

Then I heard Phill say, "Let's get out."

We did and proceeded to the bed. Lay down he said, then I heard a buzzing noise that unded like clippers.

"I wanna shave you clean."

"Sure," I said, "anything you want."

The vibration from the clippers were so erotic, it made me want him right then. After he t me bald and wiped clean, I felt him fondle my clit. I could feel his fingers go inside of me d the next thing I felt was his tongue working overtime. He devoured me like a man on death w eating his last meal.

It wasn't long after I came all over his face! He loves when I cum all over his face! I got and pushed him down to his back. I took all of him in my mouth and then I climbed on top of n and rode him like a good cowgirl. I yelled out for him to spank me and he did! I could feel body tightening up and just as he's about to cum. He pushed me forward, only to stick his ngue in my hole. It was overpowering as I could feel myself about to explode.

"Please stick it in me," I pleaded.

He did with so much force and we both exploded on one another after a few rounds!

It was amazing but for some reason, I still felt like I was missing something. I shook it o
and fell asleep.

The alarm clock went off waking me up.

"I turned to Phill and said, "Get up honey before you miss your flight. I talked to the girls
d they will be in town soon."

I helped Phill get everything together and saw him off. Then went back upstairs back to
d. It was only five a.m., so why not go back to bed and get more rest. When I woke up again, I
dn't know I slept in so late. When I turned over to look at the clock it was noon. I must have
en really tired,

I rolled out of bed, started the shower and went to press play on my CD player. I heard
yz II Men singing so sweetly in my ears. I showered and thought about Phil and I from last
ght. I missed him already and he hasn't even been gone for a day yet. Just when I was about
feel sad, the doorbell rang.

I turned the shower off and pressed the intercom and asked, "Who is it?"

Then I heard some ladies yell, "It's us."

I flipped on the cameras that Phill recently installed and saw that it was Ann and Liz. I
reamed and pressed the unlock button to let them in! I could hear the girls yelling my name. I
d them I would be right down after I got dressed.

"Make yourself at home girls."

I got dressed in one of Phill's T shirts and ran downstairs. I was so excited to see my
ter friends. We hugged and talked in the doorway until I realized they still had their luggage
th them. I showed them to their own rooms downstairs, gave them a tour of the house and
t them settled in. The feeling of having them there was unexplainable!

"So how long can you all stay?" I asked.

"Well, I took two weeks off," said Liz.

"And so did I," said Ann.

We all screamed like high school girls. I can see that this is going to be the best two
eks ever!

"So, Sha, we want to see the town and all the hot spots," said Ann.

"Well girls what do you have a taste for?"

They both yelled, "*MEN!*"

15

Okay, I have the perfect spot. We all got dressed in our sexiest dresses with heels to di for. Our hair and faces were flawless. We met up in the foyer of the house, smiled and jumped in my crème color Chevy Equinox. My husband just bought that as an I love you gift. We pulled up to **Essence**, it was a strip club featuring some of the hottest men and breathtaking women. We got a seat at the front table so we could see EVERYTHING! As we talked and drank, we we really getting relaxed.

Then we heard *Pony* by *Ginuwine* come on and this dark chocolate god appeared on stage in a cowboy get up. He had moves that would make you daydream at night. He walked over to Ann and started grinding in front of her and she was all teeth! We stayed there until one in the morning. I didn't drink much because I was the designated driver.

After returning to my house, I grabbed the phone to call Phill and tell him about our night. Our conversation veered off to the left a bit.

Then I heard Phill say, "Connect me to the video. I want to see you."

I jumped up off the bed and started connecting the wires. As soon as I saw him, I began to blush and smile.

Phill said, "Take your clothes off baby."

I began to undress, by the time I looked up he was completely naked! My mouth watered for his package. He began to rub himself from the chest down and I watched every second of it. I laid on the bed and began to rub just the tips of my nipples, that is always my weak spot. As we watched one another touch and caress, it made us both want more. I could feel me reaching my climax and then I heard Phill.

"Baby I'm almost there!"

I said, "So am I!"

We both reached the point of explosion together and then exhaled.

Phill said, "I love you Shalay and we will see each other soon."

I said, "I love you too" and blew him a kiss before hanging up the video.

I jumped into the shower, washed and went downstairs to check in on the girls only to find everyone asleep! So, I went back upstairs to get in bed.

apter 5

E SURPRISE

I jumped out of my sleep to the sound of my doorbell. I looked at the clock and it was y six a.m.

"Are you kidding," I said. "This has got to be a joke."

I put on my robe and went downstairs and snatched the door open only to see a autifully wrapped gift box on my doorstep.

"Now where did this come from?" I thought to myself.

I read the card and it said, **TO MY LOVE, THANKS FOR LAST NIGHT**! I knew immediately t it was from Phill, so I opened the box and saw a set of keys and a map. I was thrown so I ed Phill.

"Hi hunny, I really enjoyed last night too but what is this gift all about?"

"Well, it's a surprise, just follow the map," was the last thing Phill told me before he ng up.

All I could do was laugh! I went to Liz and Ann's room to wake them up for the journey were going to take today.

"Get up ladies we are pulling out at 10a.m. sharp!"

This was so exciting, I felt like a kid on a scavenger hunt. After eating breakfast and ting on my comfortable jeans and sneakers, we got in the car and followed the directions on map. We ended up on this long-paved road with trees on both sides of the road. I felt like had taken a wrong turn somewhere, but the GPS assured us we were going in the right ction. We looked up and saw this great big pond, beautiful grassy yard and a log cabin. We led up, parked and got out. I grabbed the keys went to the door and it opened. There was a e full of red and white roses with a note and envelope stuck to it.

The note read; **MY LOVE WE HAVE ALWAYS TALKED ABOUT HAVING A HOME AWAY)M HOME AND THIS IS IT!** I opened it and there was the deed to the house and property in name! I was so floored, I burst into tears. Liz, Ann and I began to hug and cry together.

I called Phill in tears and he said, "So I guess this means you like it?"

"**NO!** I love it Phill, you are the best husband in the world!"

"Oh really, am I?" Phill responded.

"**YES! YES! YES**, you are!" I replied.

Suddenly the phone got quiet. I called Phill's name more than once and no answer. Th
I felt a tap on my shoulder. I turned to see Phill standing there.

"**OH MY GOSH!** Where did you come from? When did you get here?"

"I've been here since last night! Hey Liz and Ann, I didn't leave you ladies out. I have tw
of my boys that should be arriving in ten minutes."

Ann replied, "Phill are you crazy! We are in jeans and sneakers; couldn't you have
warned us?"

"Ladies just chill the guys are down to earth and very relaxed; you both look great."

Just then, the doorbell rings.

Phill answers the door and in walks Brad and Thomas.

"Yo Phill what's going on my brother?" said Thomas "This is a nice spot man."

"Thanks man, come on in and let me introduce you to the ladies. Ann, Liz I would like
you two to meet Brad and Thomas."

In sync, they replied, "Nice to meet you!"

Phill said, "Well let's go out on the deck, I ordered lunch and it will be here in 30
minutes."

"Good that's enough time for us to go and freshen up a bit," said Sha.

"But Sha we don't have a change of clothes here," whispered Ann.

"Well, no worries ladies, go check the hall closet," smirked Phill.

Liz pulls the doors open revealing three different sundresses and three pairs of sandal
along with three personalized gift bags filled with personal feminine items.

"Wait," said Ann, "how could you possibly have known our sizes?"

"Well, I took the picture that my wife has with the three of you together with me whe
went shopping. The sales lady looked at the picture and went to work! So, if they don't fit
blame the sales lady at **Bloomingdales!**"

"Wow hunny you thought of everything," I happily said to my husband.

"You are an amazing man and that's why I love you!"

I then turned to my girls and with clapping said, "Ok ladies chop, chop! I know how lon
it takes you all to get ready!"

"The guys and I are going to have a few drinks and meet you outside," said Phill.

18

The ladies left and got ready just before the food arrived.

"Finally," said Thomas.

"You ladies are stunning," said Brad.

"Well, much thanks to **Bloomingdales**, oh and you too Phill," Liz said jokingly.

The air was warm and relaxing as it blew across the water. We sat and talked until dnight without even noticing the time.

Phill looked down at his watch and said, "Wow we have been out here a long time. lies we have to catch a 6 a.m. flight back to Hartford so we all better hit the hay."

Each couple walked hand in hand across the breezeway back to the house. Brad looked .iz and said goodnight, but she grabbed his arm and said, "Please don't leave yet."

He smiled and they went to her guest room. Thomas and Ann were already headed to room for a listen to soft jazz and whatever came next. Phill and Shalay were already in the wer together. The sweet smell of sex was all through the room. Everything was just perfect!

Chapter 6

Waking up and realizing that Phill and the guys were already gone was a bit sad. However, I knew he only had 3 more weeks away, which would leave me alone for two weeks once the girls are gone next week. I am definitely going to miss them. Well, they are here now so I will enjoy my sister friends. Too bad we haven't from Chelle in about a year. I really would love to see her and talk to her. We shared some amazing times together. She is the one thing will keep hidden, the one thing I desire often in my alone time, that one thing I secretly crave Well, that was water under the bridge.

As I got downstairs there was breakfast, juices, coffee, fresh fruits already laid out! Ph arranged everything since before his arrival, that man makes me smile continuously even whe I don't want to! I let the ladies get up on their own, slowly they came into the kitchen with big smiles on their faces. Well, I guess I don't have to ask you all how you slept! They both giggle

"OMG Sha, last night was phenomenal!" said Liz.

"Yesss it was!" added Ann. "I have not had sex like that in years. I didn't think Thomas would ever reach his climax. He was like the energizer bunny!"

All the ladies chanted, "He kept going and going and going!"

We all laughed at that.

"I have no complaints about Brad," said Liz. "The way he touched me it was like he wanted to make sure that every inch of me knew he was there! I can't wait until we link up again!"

So, I guess that means you both got their numbers."

"Of course," said the ladies.

"I ain't letting that chocolate god get away from me," said Ann.

"Right," said Liz, "I have to let Phill know he picked some winners for us!"

"Okay ladies how about we get out and do some shopping and later dinner and a movie."

Liz said, "Shopping and dinner **YES!** But a movie no."

"Why?" said Sha.

"Well, I have a surprise for you."

"Well what kind of surprise?" said Sha.

"Uh, the key word here is surprise Sha!"

"Oh, okay I can wait then. Meanwhile let's eat and then go back to my house to get dy for our day."

"This is going to be a great day, and look at this spread," said Ann. "You must have been since 5a.m. to have all of this done."

"Ohhhhh no," said Sha, "Phill had this sent over."

"That guy of yours is one of a kind Sha!" said Liz "I hope Brad and Thomas are around g enough to give us the same kind of lifestyle that you are living everyday hun!"

"Well money sticks with money ya know," I replied. "I hope they also told you that y're both engineers as well."

"Yesss hunny they did," said Liz proudly.

 "And Liz being that top female at your law firm, and Ann you being nominated as the #1 diatrician for five years straight, says a lot about who you all are. Educated, successful Black men. We are the women real men respect."

"Amen to that," said Ann.

"Well, then let's eat and get ready to leave here for our day of fun and shopping and of rse *MY SURPRISE*!"

The ladies got back to Sha's house after a day of shopping in no time, got dressed and headed out. They got back around 5p.m. They all showered and got comfortable until dinner. Liz's phone rang at approximately 6:15.

I heard her say, "Are you really? Ok, I will be right there."

Liz jumped up off the couch and said, "Sha your surprise is here!"

I said, "**WHAT ARE YOU KIDDING ME?**"

I immediately got up and went to the mirror by the door and started straightening myself up. The doorbell rang, Liz answered and in walks Chelle! My heart rate sped up so quickly, I was nervous. My mind raced with all sorts of thoughts while I stood with my hands c my mouth in awe! She was as gorgeous as the first time I laid eyes on her! She had on this nue color bodycon dress that was hugging her just right, which made me imagine her naked. She was wearing a pair of black 6-inch stilettos with a black belt.

I could instantly tell she was not wearing panties, or it could have been thongs. She ha a bra on that was holding her up just right! As I was sitting there imagining I never even heard Liz calling my name. When I snapped out of it Chelle had her arms open wide to embrace me, but all of me was saying grab her and kiss those nice pouty lips!

"Oh my gosh, I am sorry excuse me for staring but I am so surprised and glad to see yo here! Come in, please!"

I turned and asked, "Liz how did you find Chelle?"

"Find her? She was never lost. We have been in contact with one another for years, since we left college. I never told you because she wanted to surprise you and by the looks of she certainly succeeded!"

"Yes, she did," said Sha, "I actually thought about you this morning. How long are you town for? Where are you staying?"

"Well, I am in town for three weeks. I took some time off. I couldn't come last week w the ladies because I had three houses to show first. I did that and now I am here to hang out with you all. I am staying at the *Holiday Inn and Suites*."

"Are you kidding?" said Sha. "Call and cancel that reservation, I wouldn't dare let you stay in a stuffy hotel for three weeks. We have more than enough room here. Come on let me show you where you can put your stuff."

Sha took Chelle up to the only guest room upstairs across from the master bedroom.

"**WOW** this is beautiful Sha!"

"Thank you I never let anyone in here, I just store shoes and clothes in the closet, so be eful when you open that side closet door!"

They both laughed!

"Okay I will let you get settled in and meet you downstairs."

"Okay, and thanks, Sha it's really good to see you."

"It's good to see you too Chelle."

After returning downstairs, I just smiled at Liz and said, "You are a great friend."

"Well, I try to be to you, all you have been to me all these years," said Liz!

"Well Ann how much did you know?"

"Well, Chelle and I talk often and I knew she would be here. I just hope she wants no ts of Thomas!"

"Seriously is that all you can think of, is sex?"

"Yessssss!" said Ann.

They all laughed!!

"Well, I am super glad that the gang is all here together again. Just like back in the day," I Sha!

Chapter 7

Dinner and drinks were great. We tried the new **Hibachi and Grill** restaurant not too far out in the city. We all rode in Chelle's Lexus LS450. I rode up front to give her directions to the spot, but it was really to watch her legs and thighs as she changed gears while driving. Anyway as we headed back to the house, I turned on some soft R&B as I walked into the door, poured glass of champagne for the four of us. Something I rarely did was drink champagne, but right now I needed something to ease my mind flow.

The ladies and I decided to make it a sleepover PJ style type of night. Really it was Ann idea, so we went and changed into some sexy lingerie and met back in the den. By coincidenc we were all wearing black and looking **_GOOD_** I might add! **_MAN_**, if the guys could see us now, then in walks Chelle she was **_BREATHTAKINGLY BEAUTIFUL_**! We were all shoeless because my carpeting was all white and so was the furniture. We sat on the floor and talked like we never left one another. Everything was absolutely great! Soon everyone started retiring to their bed

Chelle left first after getting in late with little sleep. About 45 minutes later we all decided to call it a night. As I climbed the stairs, I couldn't help but to peek in on Chelle. She was laying on top of the covers still in her nighty, fast asleep. So of course, I walked in to throw a blanket over her, after all I kept the temp in the house at 69, so this is the right thing to do right? That's what I kept telling myself after peeping over the balcony to make sure Liz and An were asleep. After seeing it was dark and quiet, I went on in to cover Chelle. As I put the blank over her, she moaned in her sleep and then turned over to her back.

My eyes went straight to those size 44 mounds sitting up and looking so perky.

After she felt the covers on her she opened her eyes smiled up at me and said, "Thanks."

I said, "You're welcome," and proceeded to leave.

Chelle reached out and grabbed my hand and said, "No, don't leave, stay with me tonight."

I said, "Chelle I can't we are in my husband's house along with Liz and Ann downstairs

She said, "I've missed you and I so much. I have been longing for you and your touch years."

I said, "Same here," as I sat on the edge of the bed.

I then reached out to touch her hair that was cut into a short sexy bob. We began to k with so much passion that I lost myself in her love. I could not wait to put my mouth on those 44's as she grabbed and rubbed on my butt. I reached around and untied her nighty, I watche as it slowly fell off her shoulders, dropped to the bed and revealed just what my mouth was drooling for. As I leaned in and took in as much of the right one as my mouth could take, I

24

essed the left. I could hear her moan with pleasure. I then grabbed them both and inhaled
‑ soft scent. Her hand went into my panties on both sides and slid them off with ease. I felt
‑ warm palm as it touched my girly parts. She rubbed, fingered and massaged as I did the
me in returned to her.

Oh, how I've missed this girl so much, I craved her taste, her aroma, her touch. I laid her
wn and licked her from head to toe and as my face reached her intimate part, I could smell
hot aroma and see her wetness of wanting. I could not wait to take her in my mouth.
ALLY, after years of missing Chelle I was in her secret garden and pleasing her as if it were
‑ first time together. She began to grind on my face holding my head in place so that I could
te all of her. After a while she exploded in my mouth and on my face. It was like sweet wine
he taste!

She got up and pushed me with force on my back to the bed and said, "my turn!"

All it took was for her to touch my clit and then she inserted one finger, then two then
REE. Hey, Phill and I are regular sooo that was expected but she touched me with such love,
‑ntion and devotion and all I could do was wish we could stay in this position forever. She
ked on my breast and pleased me until I couldn't take it anymore and I released all over her
‑le she held me tightly in place as if she didn't want one drop to spill out of her mouth. After
‑hing my breath, we got into the 69 and started to take in one another.

We grinded...

...moaned...

...and pleased each other until we were full of each other's love potion. Soon, we drifted
to sleep in one another's arm.

The loud alarm sounded off again. I jumped up out of my sleep to see that it was 4a.m.,
‑ I quickly ran back to my room as Chelle turned over. As I got in bed, I realized that sleep
‑ so far away from my mind. I just laid there and thought about what had taken place with
‑lle and I. The thoughts played over and over again in my head continuously. How could we
‑or hours and still want more of each other. Then I began to think about Phill and realized
‑t after his first nut he was in sleep land without hesitation, leaving me wanting more. Don't
‑me wrong he could handle his business in bed but I would always feel like there was more I
‑ted and could take.

In that moment that's when I realized that my *more* was my hidden desire and my
‑len desire was across the hall from me. I began to smile because my body was telling me to
‑et some more but my mind was telling me to slow down and take it easy. Of course, my
‑y won that fight, so I slowly sneaked back over to Chelle's room and I didn't care that she
‑ asleep, I could still smell her on me, so I went in to my *more* mode and got some more. I
‑ right in and buried my face into her wonderland. I sucked and licked as she grabbed my
‑d (which I secretly loved) and she came all over my face. I enjoyed every moment of it, I left

25

her there wanting more of me, as I walked out, I turned to see her pleasing herself, I just smile and kept walking away.

I jumped in the shower and began to wash our love making away. As I washed myself, began to rub and rub until my hands were soaked from my juices. Hey this shower was gonna take longer than I expected as I smiled to myself. After finally getting dressed, I went downstairs only to find everyone in the kitchen cooking breakfast.

Liz asked, "What would you like Sha?"

As soon as I was about to respond Chelle looked in my direction,

I said, "Uhhh ahh just fresh fruits, waffles and eggs please."

When what I really wanted was to have Chelle on a platter!

Chelle asked, "So, Sha can I ask you a question, it's kinda a personal matter that I need your professional service in."

"Okay sure, we can go over to my office where we can have a little privacy. Don't worry won't bill you this time!"

"Ladies we will be back in about an hour, is that all right."

"Well, its fine," said Liz. "I have some paperwork to have completed before I get back work from this vacay anyway."

"So, do I," said Ann, "I need to call my sub and get some info on my patients."

"Thanks ladies," I replied.

Chelle and I got dressed and I told her when she was ready, to walk across the bridge my office. Usually, I charge a pretty penny for my counseling but Chelle paid me in full last nig and early this morning. I had on my floral print skirt and white button up shirt with my notepa in hand I prepared myself for the session.

A knock came to the door,

"Come in," I said.

Chelle walked in with an all-white knee length summer dress, hair curled neatly with little to no makeup which she really didn't need anyway on her soft smooth skin. She was looking so sexy and my mind was about to veer off.

"Snap out of it Sha," I had to tell myself.

Come in Michelle, have a seat here on the couch. I tell all my clients to take their shoe off lay back and relax. As Michelle laid there, she began to go into details about her personal experiences that she has been having with men and wondering why she could not keep a ma

und long. She was always concerned about some childhood experiences that took place that
e never addressed and because of that, she would rather not have a man around no matter
w hard she tried. She told me about the relationship with Eric the three years that they were
ether and how their lovemaking always made her think about a particular lady. She didn't
a name or anything but Sha could understand her totally.

"So, Michelle is there a reason why you haven't addressed the situations?"

"Well, I never felt the need to address them at first. But for whatever reason I keep
ting these flashbacks of the terrible things that happened."

"And this particular woman you have been wanting is a prime example of what you
lly want. It's a hidden desire that you may need to address in some way shape or form. And
ause you made the decision to bypass what has taken place in your past the thoughts will
tinue to haunt you until you do."

After our one-hour session as I do with all my patients. I told Chelle to relax as we went
ough a mind exercise. She performed the exercise without any problems and her mind
an to stand still. After the buzzer went off, I told Michelle that anytime she needed to talk
t I would be there for her. So, she made an appointment for the next week Friday and every
Jay for the next two months. I told her it was ok but, was she fine with being my patient.

She said, "Of course and I have no problem paying the fees either."

I said, "Okay."

We signed the contracts and I thanked her. Then Michelle turns to me and asks, "Is the
tor out or in?"

I said, "Which one do you need me to be?"

She said, "Out."

I said, "Well, she is out."

"Good," Chelle said. "You didn't think I was going to let you get away with this morning,
you?"

Chelle pushed me down on the couch in my office that was against the wall. I never
erstood why I had that couch there. I always only have one patient at a time in here, my
ointments never lapse and its certainly not a waiting room. But from the looks of it, I was
ut to find the purpose for it. Michelle unbuttoned my shirt while gazing into my eyes. She
an to kiss my lips, then my neck. She took my size 40's right into her mouth with such ease
passion while reaching under my skirt only to find out I wasn't wearing any panties.

She smiled and got down on her knees and began to kiss on my pearl until I was soaking
, her tongue did wonders! For the next 35 minutes we took turns pleasuring one another.

Then we walked back to the house only to find Ann and Liz still working. I quietly went into Phill's home office and ordered lunch for us. We all had different kinds of salads and wine. W ate and talked and they never even knew what just took place with Chelle and I. It was great like an adrenaline rush and I enjoyed every minute of it.

The time had wound down and the ladies were all preparing to leave. Ann and Liz had a ,ht back to LA at 6a.m. and Chelle wasn't leaving until Sunday morning.

"It's our last night together ladies what should we do?" I asked them

Liz suggested the strip club and we all agreed. After getting dressed we went out to ve a blast! As we walked *The Strip* (that's what we call it here in Myrtle Beach), we saw a sign a building that said *X-TA-SEE*! That name alone made us want to go in for sure! We grabbed eat at the bar, ordered drinks and waited patiently for the show. The music started and a y tall 6'4 vanilla drink got on the stage and started our night out so lovely! We yelled, ghed and even threw money.

We stayed until midnight and wanted to stay longer but we knew the ladies had to leave : so early in the morning. Once we returned to the house showered and relaxed, we all fell eep in my bedroom, it was like high school all over again. I was awoken by the sound of an rm clock. I promised to drive my sister friends to the airport, so I got up left Chelle asleep d drove them. We hugged and cried, I told them how much I was gonna miss them and hed they were much closer.

Ann replies, "Hey you never know how things will turn out with the guys."

"Let's cross our fingers on that one and hope for the best."

I stayed with them until they boarded their flights. Then I headed back home, hoping to more rest. Only when I got back, I found Chelle wide awoke and completely naked.

I smiled and said, "Not here, after all it is my husband's bed as well."

We walked across the hall back to the guest room that Chelle was using, my heart began ace with joy and excitement. As I watched her walk to the bed, I was getting so excited vn below. She got up on the bed on her hands and knees and looked back at me. The view s so inviting and luscious. Without hesitation I spanked her behind and put my face in the ce right where she wanted it. I could smell her heat and see the juices already dripping that I : loved tasting. I held her so tight and close so that she could receive all of me. That's when I lized I have a special place in my heart for her that no one could ever fill or remove.

Sunday morning came so quickly and it was time for Chelle to leave. The best part about ough is that she only lives an hour away and I never knew this. We talked and talked while I ched her pack for her departure. She started loading her car and we started to walk around ny yard until we ended up in what she has told me is her favorite spot, my office. Thank god chairs were leather because we were really getting it all wet. We pleasured each other so

5

long until we remembered that she had a time to get back home and get back to work. After she had some houses to get sold soon as possible.

We walked back to the main house and Chelle turned to me and said, "Do you know that you are my one true **hidden desire** and I love you!"

All I could say was "**WOW!**" and watched her drive off in her car.

As I walked back inside, I looked around at the now empty house and began to think about all the fun we had for these past few weeks. I love my sister friends without a doubt and was glad for the time spent.

I started to clean up a bit before the housekeeper got there. After all I didn't want any evidence of my actions to be reported to my husband. After all she told him everything. I was beginning to think she has a thing for him. I can recall the day I came in from my office and she never heard me enter the house. She was wiping my husband's face with a napkin every time he took a bite of food. She was even massaging his neck. I stood and watched and I just cleared my throat not once but twice. Eventually she turned to see me standing there hands on my hip and waiting for an explanation.

HIDDEN DESIRES PART 2
THE HOUSEKEEPER

Phill and I had just bought our new home and we were both professional workers so eping this big thing would be a task. We sat and discussed getting a housekeeper and doing me interviews.

"Shalay put an ad out for the housekeeper please," said Phill.

"Okay hunny no problem."

After getting the ad out we started receiving calls for interviews. We talked to 5 ferent ladies and Phill didn't like any of them but when Lisa came in, he sat up in his seat and iled the whole time we interviewed her.

He then said, "Okay we will get back to you"

Once she left, all I could hear was, "Babe she is the one."

I asked, "Well what made her so fit for the position? All you did was smile the whole e she sat there."

"Come on Shalay I believe she can handle the job."

So, I agreed and we hired her and called her back and asked her when she could start. said Monday will be fine, we agreed and hung up. Monday came in and she showed up for k in her little maids uniform and heels. I quickly said no heels on the floor dear, you have to comfortable for all the walking and cleaning you will be doing, I did notice how sexy she was ch is probably the same thing Phill was seeing in the interview.

Lisa said, "Yes ma'am but I didn't bring any other shoes."

"What size do you wear?" I asked

"A nine," she said.

So, I led her upstairs to my room.

As she entered, I heard Lisa said wow, "This is beautiful."

"Thanks, I said and opened my closet and handed her a pair of flats from my stash of es.

"Well since we are already upstairs, I can go ahead and give you a tour of the house."

Made in the USA
Middletown, DE
19 May 2022

65955753R00018